# CONTENTS

Mina thinks people taste like dirty socks, so beetroot juice is her snack of choice. Its red colour has fooled her parents into thinking that she's a traditional blood-sucking vampire instead of a superhero. She has the ability to change into a bat or a mouse at will.

Brian is the brainy one amongst his friends. Unlike other zombies, Brian prefers tofu to brains. No matter what sort of trouble is brewing, Brian always comes up with a plan to save the day, like a true superhero.

# BRIAN *(the Zombie)*

# WILL (the Ghost)

Will is quite shy. Luckily he can become invisible whenever he wants to, because he is a ghost. When Will is doing good deeds, he likes to remain unseen. His invisibility helps him to be brave like a real superhero.

With a wave of her wand and a poetic chant, Linda can reverse any magical curse. She hopes to use her magic to help people, just like a superhero would.

# LINDA (the Witch)

# CHAPTER 1

# HARRIET

*BRRRIIINGGG!!!*

Classes at Frankenstein Primary School were about to start. Ghouls and ghosts floated across the playground. Ogres and orcs stomped towards the front steps. Monsters of all sorts rushed through the doors.

Brian nervously watched. He took a deep breath.

"Okay, you can do this," he told himself.

Brian was clever. He liked school. No, he *loved* school. He was a person who asked for homework every night. His classmates found that really annoying.

But something on the other side of those school doors scared him. Her name was Harriet Lycoan. Harriet was a werewolf. She was part human and part wolf.

In the sky above, a full moon shone. Brian glanced up at it and shivered in fear.

"Oh great," he said. "It's going to be a bad night of school."

Brian took another deep breath. Then he joined the group of monsters entering the school. He hoped he would just blend in.

But he was not that lucky.

A hairy hand grabbed Brian's shoulder. It yanked him backwards.

"It's Brainy Brian!" Harriet said. "How's it going, *Foul Meat*?"

Behind Brian's hairy bully stood a werecat called Kitty and a feathery werebird called Polly. They were all half human and half animal.

"Foul Meat! Foul Meat!" Polly repeated. "Ha! Because he's a zombie."

Just as Brian was about to become lunch meat, Kitty grumbled, "Who is that?"

Through the doors walked a strange-looking mummy.

"It's a new kid," Harriet growled.

"Some *old meat*," Kitty snarled.

"Ha! Old meat! Old meat!" Polly repeated. "Because he's a mummy!"

Harriet let go of Brian. He fell to the ground with a thud.

"We're gonna have some fun with the new kid after school," Harriet snarled.

When the bullies had walked away, Brian went to his classroom.

# CHAPTER 2

# THE NEW KID

During computer lessons, Brian sat next to his friend Will.

"Have you seen the new kid?" Brian asked. "He's a mummy."

"Boys can't be mummies," Will said.

Brian rolled his eyes.

"*Mummy*. Not *mummy*," he said.

Next, Brian had languages with his friend Linda.

She was chanting a poem. "Eye of newt and toe of frog, wool of bat and tongue of dog," she said.

As Brian sat down next to her, Linda asked, "Did you memorize your chant for today? It's a really fun one."

Of course he had. Brian always did his homework. But something else was on his mind.

"Have you seen the new kid?" he asked Linda. "He's a mummy."

"Yeah, I saw him with Mina," Linda replied.

Mina was a vampire. Like Will and Linda, she was one of Brian's best friends.

After the lesson, Brian found Mina in the canteen. She was sitting with the new kid. Will and Linda were also there.

Brian sat down with his friends. He looked from the new kid to Mina. Something was weird.

"Hey! Is this toilet paper?" Brian asked.

"Maybe," the new kid muttered.

"Are you a human wrapped in toilet paper?" Brian asked.

"Yeah," Mina said, blushing. "It's my neighbour Greg."

"I wanted to come to school with Mina tonight," Greg said.

"Well, now you're in serious trouble," Brian said.

Brian told his friends about the werebullies.

Most monsters thought it
was funny to scare people. But
not Brian and his friends. They
wanted to be like superheroes.
They wanted to save the day and
help people.

"What are we going to do?"
Will asked.

"We can't let those bullies hurt
Greg," Mina said.

"Yeah, I don't want to be an
after-school snack," Greg said.

"We won't let you become bully
bait," Mina said.

"Mina, you've given me an
idea," Brian said.

# THE SUPER SUN

After their last lesson, the friends met by the front doors.

"Everyone know the plan?" Brian asked.

Everyone nodded.

With a *POOF!* Mina turned into a bat. Will dropped his sheet and disappeared.

Then Greg stepped outside. Mina and Will ducked behind him.

The three werebullies were waiting.

"Hey, it's snack time," Harriet snarled.

"Snack time! Snack time!" Polly repeated. "Because we're–"

"You need to stop that!" Kitty grumbled.

"It is really annoying," Harriet growled.

As the bullies argued, Will and Mina grabbed Greg's toilet-paper wrappings. They whirled around, pulling the wrappings off. Then they whirled around, wrapping up the bullies instead.

"Hey, what are you doing?" Polly squawked.

"It's just toilet paper," Kitty grumbled.

"Hey, he's just a boy," Harriet snarled at Greg. "Let's eat!"

Before the bullies could do anything, Linda burst through the doors. She waved her wand in the air and chanted, "Bullies become undone under a bright yellow sun."

And *POOF!*

Instead of night-time, it was daytime. Instead of a full moon, the sun shone overhead.

"Oh no!" Harriet and the bullies shouted.

One by one, they went missing. *POOF! POOF! POOF!*

The werebullies were now just three kids wrapped in toilet paper.

Then it was Brian's turn. He stepped outside and held his arms in front of him.

"Brains!" he groaned. "Brains!"

He lumbered towards the bullies.

"Brains! Brains!" Polly squawked. "He's going to eat our brains!"

The bullies got up and ran away.

"Ha, if only they had half a brain," Mina said.

"They'd know Brian prefers meatballs," Will said.

Brian high-fived Linda.

"We saved the day!" he said.

"Just like real superheroes," Linda said.

## DAVE BARDIN

Dave Bardin studied illustration while working as an art teacher. As an artist, Dave has worked on many different projects for television, books, comics and animation. In his spare time Dave enjoys watching documentaries, listening to podcasts, travelling and spending time with friends and family.

## BLAKE HOENA

Blake A. Hoena grew up in Wisconsin, USA, where he wrote stories about robots conquering the Moon and trolls lumbering around the woods behind his house. He now lives in Minnesota, USA, and continues to write about fun things such as space aliens and superheroes. Blake has written more than fifty chapter books and graphic novels for children.

# GLOSSARY

**bait** food used as a trap for catching animals

**chant** say a phrase again and again

**foul** unpleasant or disgusting

**ghoul** evil spirit

**lumber** move at a slow pace

**memorize** learn by heart

**orc** mythical creature

**snarl** growl, usually showing teeth

**whirl** move around quickly in a circle

# THINK ABOUT IT

**1.** Bullies are scarier than monsters! What would you do if you were having problems with a bully?

**2.** If you could choose between being a vampire, a witch, a ghost or a zombie, which would you choose to be? Why?

**3.** Brian and his friends don't want to scare people; they want to be like superheroes and help people. If you could be a superhero, how would you help people?

# WRITE ABOUT IT

1. Write a list of the lessons you think Brian has in one day. What subjects do you think they teach at Frankenstein Primary School?

2. Greg uses a toilet-paper disguise to sneak into school with Mina. Write about a day that Mina sneaks into Greg's school. What do you think might happen?

3. Write a paragraph about a time when you have been "the new kid", (whether on a sports team, at a school or with a group of friends). Try to use as many details as possible to capture what you were feeling.

# THE FUN DOESN'T STOP HERE!

Discover more at
www.raintree.co.uk